GERALDINE

Elizabeth Lilly

A NEAL PORTER BOOK
ROARING BROOK PRESS
NEW YORK

To Shadra for many cheers and helping hands,
to SPH for a light in the dark,
and to Nancy, Jim, Margaret, Julia, and Anayah
for being on my team always and forever.
Mil gracias, a thousand thank-yous.
You all helped me get here.

Copyright © 2018 by Elizabeth Liilly
A Neal Porter Book
Published by Roaring Brook Press
Roaring Brook Press is a division of Holtzbrinck Publishing Holdings Limited Partnership
175 Fifth Avenue, New York, NY 10010
The art for this book was created using using pen-and-ink and watercolor, then edited and compiled digitally.
mackids.com

Library of Congress Control Number: 2017957292
ISBN: 978-1-62672-359-7

Our books may be purchased in bulk for promotional, educational, or business use. Please
contact your local bookseller or the Macmillan Corporate and Premium Sales Department
at (800) 221-7945 ext. 5442 or by e-mail at MacmillanSpecialMarkets@macmillan.com.

First edition, 2018
Printed in China by RR Donnelley Asia Printing Solutions Ltd.,
Dongguan City, Guangdong Province
10 9 8 7 6 5 4 3 2 1

I'm moving.

It is the Worst Thing Ever.

PRO | CON
I | ~~IIII~~ ~~IIII~~
| ~~IIII~~ ~~IIII~~
II |

"Geraldine, what did I tell you about being a drama queen?" says Mom.

"Just think of it as
a Grand Adventure!"
says Dad.

"NO!" I say.
"No, no,
no, no, no,
NO, NO . . .

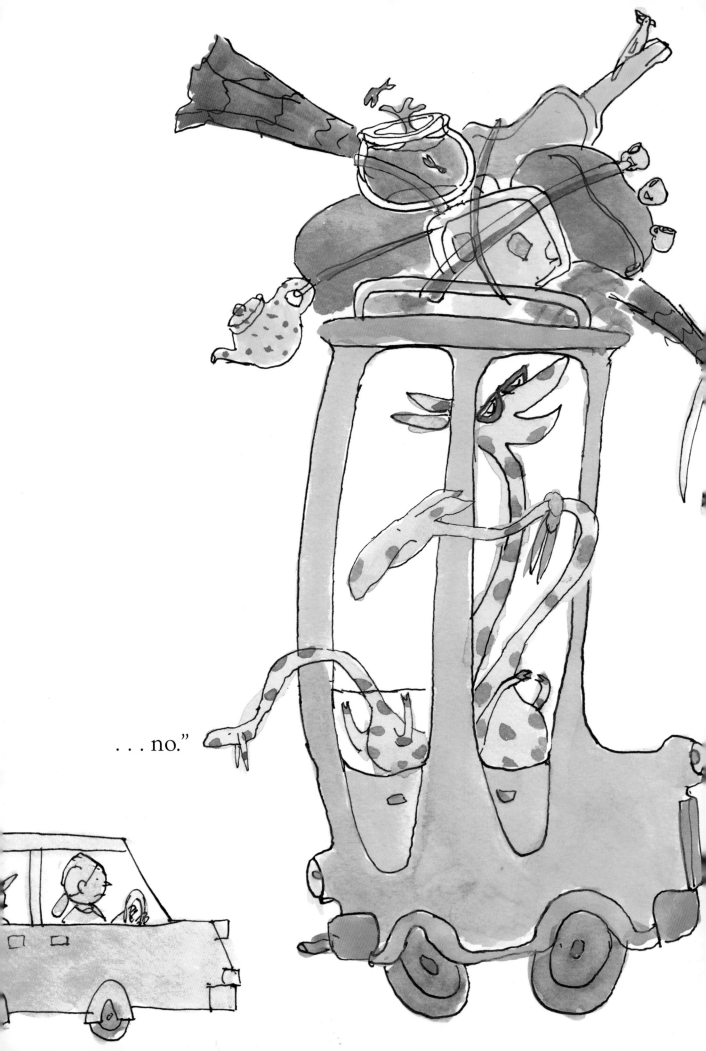

. . . no."

On Monday morning,
Mom goes to her new job.

Dad walks me to school.

I learn two things before school even starts:

One, I am *definitely* the
only giraffe in this school.

And two, flags make very good handkerchiefs.

In Giraffe City, I felt like Geraldine.

But here,
I just feel like That Giraffe Girl.

I'm shy, which I never
was before.
It turns out
when you are
my height,
hiding is
not easy.

Even my voice
tries to hide;
it's gotten quiet
and *whispery*.

One day, someone is in my lunch hiding spot.
I notice her food is organized like this:

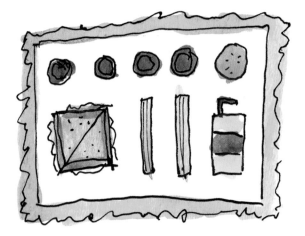

"Who are you?" I ask.

"I bet you've heard of me," she says,
and she sounds kind of mad.
"I'm that girl who wears glasses
and likes MATH and
always organizes
her food!"

"No—no, I meant your name," I say.

"Oh," she says.

"It's Cassie."

We decide to hide together. It's fun.

"You know, Cassie," I say one day. "You are not just some girl who does unusual stuff. You are Cassie! You make up fantabulous games! You're nice! You can do a handstand for 167 seconds! I think you are Really Great."

"You know," she says to me, kind of quiet. "You are not just a giraffe. You're Geraldine. You dance like crazy. You pretend so well, one time I thought you were the Queen of England. You are the one and only Geraldine, and I think you are Really Great, too."

I think about this, and my head stands up a little taller.

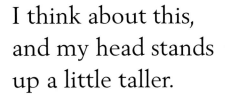

The next day, I drag Cassie to the lunch table.
"We are Really Great, remember?" I tell her.

(She does not seem to remember.)

"This is CASSIE!!" I say, really loud,
so my voice will stop hiding.
"Cassie can stay in a handstand for 167 seconds."

"Reeeally??" says Melinda Bucket,
and I can tell she is very impressed.

"And this is GERALDINE!" says Cassie, nice and loud.
(She's not letting her voice hide, either.)
Then Cassie says, "Geraldine is the Queen of England."

Everyone looks at me.

Oh no, oh no no no—

"Why, of course I am, daaahhhling," I finally say,
with my most queenly royal wave.

And everyone laughs. In a good way.
Me and Cassie and Melinda Bucket and everyone
all laugh together for the rest of lunch that day.
And the next day! And the next!

Little by little, I think everyone forgets
I was That Giraffe Girl,

including me.

Now Cassie and I
still hide,

but only when we're
playing hide-and-seek.

It's still hard to fit into things.

In the school play,
I am Tree Number Two.

And when we go camping, I get a LOT of fresh air.
People still look at me funny sometimes,
and sometimes I want to hide,
or go home, or cry.

But almost all of the time I know
that I am more than That Giraffe Girl,
I am the one and only Geraldine—

and I am Really Great.